Bob the Builder™

Travis Paints the Town

BBC

It was a busy morning in Bob's building yard. Wendy had a long list of jobs that had to be done that day.

"Right then, Bob," she called. "You, Muck and Roley are off to finish that new section of the town road. Travis will follow you with the road-marking machine in his trailer."

"What's a road-marking machine?" asked Muck.

"It's a special machine that paints lines down the middle of a new road," Bob explained. "Cars travel on either side of the line so that they don't bump into each other."

"It's ever so important to keep the line straight," added Wendy.

The team set off for the new section of road. When they got there, Roley thundered up and down, flattening every bump in sight.

"Nearly finished!" he called across to Bob, who was unloading the road-marking machine.

"Good," said Bob. "Then I can start painting the road."

The busy machines did not notice that Spud was peeping at them from behind a bush in a nearby field. When he saw what they were doing, he gave a big grin.

"This looks like a lot of fun!" he chuckled.

Bob pushed the road-marking machine into the middle of the road and loaded it with thick white paint. He was just about to start painting lines, when his mobile phone rang.

"Hello, Mrs Potts!" he said. "What can I do for you? Really? No, don't worry, I'll pop over right away!"

"What's up, Bob?" rumbled Roley.

"Mrs Potts's fence is broken and she doesn't want her dog to get out onto the road," Bob replied. "I'd better go over there. It won't take me long to fix it."

"OK, Bob, we'll wait here," said Roley.

"I'll be back in a jiffy!" shouted Bob,
as he jumped onto Muck and
roared off down the road.
Travis, Roley and Bird
stood in the sunshine, waiting
for Bob to come back. They didn't see Spud
pop up from behind a bush and creep towards the road-
marking machine. Very quietly, he dragged the machine
behind Travis. Then the mischievous scarecrow unhooked the
empty trailer – and attached the road-marking machine in its
place! Then he slipped back to the bushes.

"Tee-hee!" he giggled. "Now, for some fun!"

Spud walked out, whistling loudly, as if he had just arrived. "Hi, Travis!" he called. "I've got a message for you! Farmer Pickles wants you down at the pond. It's *really* important."

"I'd better get going," said Travis.

He roared off, pulling the road-marking machine behind him!

As Travis hurried on his way, the road-marking machine bounced along after him, painting wiggly lines all over the new road.

"Har-har," chortled Spud, as he inspected the wet white paint.

"Stop, Travis! Come back!" Roley bellowed when he saw what was happening. "Come on, Bird! We can't just stand here and watch Travis make a mess of Bob's new road. We've got to stop him!"

"**Wheeee!**" whistled Bird.

From behind the bush, naughty Spud rocked with laughter as Roley lumbered off after Travis.

"This is the best fun ever!" laughed Spud.

Travis hurried to the duck pond as fast as his wheels could turn. He didn't look left or right as he rushed on his way to help Farmer Pickles.

And that was why the little tractor didn't spot Farmer Pickles working in a field next to the country lane! Travis whizzed straight past him.

"Oh, dear!" gasped Farmer Pickles when he saw the wiggly white lines trailing behind Travis. And then Roley and Bird rolled up.

"Roley! Roley!" called Farmer Pickles. **"Follow that tractor!"**

15

Wendy was in her office when Farmer Pickles phoned.
"Dear me, white paint everywhere!" she cried. "Don't worry, I'll tell Bob right away!"

Bob was busy hammering the last nail back into Mrs Potts's fence. **BANG! BANG! BANG!**
"There you go," he said. "That should keep your dog nice and safe!"
"Oh, thank you," said Mrs Potts, smiling with relief.
"No problem," said Bob, as his mobile phone rang.
"Hi, Wendy. What? Travis? Paint *everywhere*? I'm on my way!"

Travis was a lot lighter than Roley and a lot faster too! The poor steamroller panted and spluttered as he trundled along after Travis with Farmer Pickles and Bird on board.

"Oh, please stop…" Roley groaned.

"**Tra-vis!**" yelled Farmer Pickles, at the top of his voice. But Travis still couldn't hear them over the roar of his engine.

He raced along the road and disappeared around a corner. And as he went faster and faster, the white lines he painted were wigglier and wigglier!

While Roley and Farmer Pickles struggled to catch up with Travis, Bob and Muck were chasing frantically after him too.

"Quick as you can," urged Bob. "We've got to stop him before he paints the whole town white!"

"I'm already in top gear!" spluttered Muck as he revved up his engine. "I don't think I can go any faster!"

"Try, Muck," cried Bob. "Please try!"

Travis zoomed along the road and started to head across a field towards the duck pond. Spud peeped out from behind the bush to admire the mess.

"Hee-hee-hee!" he chuckled. "Now Travis is painting the grass white, too!"

Then poor, tired Roley wheezed past him. His heavy machinery clattered and rattled as he trundled after Travis.

"**Aaaarghh!**" he wailed, as Travis bounced out of sight.

Spud chased after them, laughing all the way.

Bob and Muck raced down the hill, towards the duck pond at the bottom. Bob got a terrible fright when he saw Travis heading straight for them.

"Watch out, Muck!" he yelled.

Muck tried to avoid the runaway tractor. He slammed on his brakes and screeched to a stop.

"Help!" roared Travis, swerving sideways.

One of his hub caps fell off the wheel and flew through the air. The line-marker zig-zagged behind him, then suddenly came unhooked.

It rolled down the road, skidded sideways and turned over…

Thick white paint spilled everywhere! Farmer Pickles and Roley were next to arrive. Everyone stared at the puddle of wet paint.

"Just look at this mess," Bob groaned.

Poor Travis was very upset.

"It really, really wasn't my fault, Bob," he cried. "I didn't know the line-marking machine was hooked onto me. I don't even know how it got there!"

"I tried my best to stop him, Bob," panted Roley. "But I couldn't catch him."

"Where were you going, anyway?" said Farmer Pickles.

"Spud told me you needed me right away," said Travis.

"I never said that!" exclaimed Farmer Pickles.

Behind them, a bush started to shake with laughter.

"Spud!" yelled Farmer Pickles.

Spud peeped nervously over the bush.

"What have you been up to?" Farmer Pickles asked.

"Me? Nothing!" Spud replied, trying to look innocent.

"So who hooked the line-marker onto Travis?" Bob demanded.

Spud hung his head. "Um… it *was* me," he confessed. "It was just a bit of fun. I didn't mean any harm."

Farmer Pickles glared at the naughty scarecrow.

"You've got some cleaning up to do," he said crossly. He went and got a big bucket, filled it with soapy water and gave Spud a big scrubbing brush.

"Off you go," he said. "And keep scrubbing until you've cleaned up all the paint."

"For everybody else, it's home time," called Bob.

Spud scrubbed and... scrubbed... and scrubbed. On his aching knees, he followed the wiggly lines all the way around the town, then along the country lanes.

By the time Spud finished, it was night-time. There wasn't a trace of white paint anywhere. Spud set off home.

"Can Spud scrub it?"
he said to himself.
"YES, HE CAN!"

THE
END!